W9-AST-383

Dear Parent:
Your child's love of reading starts here!

Every child learns to read in a different way and at his or her own speed. You can help your young reader improve and become more confident by encouraging his or her own interests and abilities. You can also guide your child's spiritual development by reading stories with biblical values and Bible stories, like I Can Read! books published by Zonderkidz. From books your child reads with you to the first books he or she reads alone, there are I Can Read! books for every stage of reading:

SHARED READING
Basic language, word repetition, and whimsical illustrations, ideal for sharing with your emergent reader.

BEGINNING READING
Short sentences, familiar words, and simple concepts for children eager to read on their own.

READING WITH HELP
Engaging stories, longer sentences, and language play for developing readers.

READING ALONE
Complex plots, challenging vocabulary, and high-interest topics for the independent reader.

ADVANCED READING
Short paragraphs, chapters, and exciting themes for the perfect bridge to chapter books.

I Can Read! books have introduced children to the joy of reading since 1957. Featuring award-winning authors and illustrators and a fabulous cast of beloved characters, I Can Read! books set the standard for beginning readers.

A lifetime of discovery begins with the magical words **"I Can Read!"**

Visit www.icanread.com for information on enriching your child's reading experience.
Visit www.zonderkidz.com for more Zonderkidz I Can Read! titles.

If the Lord is the one and only God, follow him.
1 Kings 18:21 NIrV

ZONDERKIDZ

Elijah and King Ahab
Copyright © 2011 by Crystal Bowman
Illustrations © 2011 by Valerie Sokolova

Requests for information should be addressed to:
Zonderkidz, *Grand Rapids, Michigan 49530*

Library of Congress Cataloging-in-Publication Data

Bowman, Crystal.
      Elijah and King Ahab / story by Crystal Bowman ; illustrated by Valerie Sokolova.
         p. cm. — (I can read! Bible stories)
      ISBN 978-0-310-72675-3 (softcover)
      1. Elijah (Biblical prophet)—Juvenile literature. 2. Ahab, King of Isreal—Juvenile literature.
3. Baal (Deity)—Juvenile literature. 4. Bible stories, English—O.T. Kings, 1st. I. Sokolova, Valerie, ill.
II. Title.
      BS580.E4B665 2012
      222'.5309505—dc23
                                              2011017062

Scriptures taken from the Holy Bible, *New International Reader's Version®, NIrV®.* Copyright© 1995,
1996, 1998 by Biblica, Inc.™ Used by permission. All rights reserved worldwide.

Any Internet addresses (websites, blogs, etc.) and telephone numbers in this book are offered as
a resource. They are not intended in any way to be or imply an endorsement by Zondervan, nor
does Zondervan vouch for the content of these sites and numbers for the life of this book.

All rights reserved. No part of this publication may be reproduced, stored in a retrieval system, or
transmitted in any form or by any means—electronic, mechanical, photocopy, recording, or any
other—except for brief quotations in printed reviews, without the prior permission of the publisher.

Zonderkidz is a trademark of Zondervan.

Editor: Mary Hassinger
Art Direction: Jody Langley

Printed in China

12 13 14 15 16 17 /DSC/ 10 9 8 7 6 5 4 3 2

ZONDERkidz

I Can Read!

BEGINNING READING 1

Elijah and King Ahab

story by Crystal Bowman
pictures by Valerie Sokolova

Elijah was a man who loved God.

One day, God said to Elijah,

"Go see King Ahab.

Tell him I will soon send rain."

So Elijah went to see King Ahab.

It had not rained in three years.

Everything had dried up.

The people did not have much food

to eat or water to drink.

Ahab was not happy to see Elijah.

"This trouble is because of you!"

said King Ahab.

"I did not give you trouble,"

said Elijah.

"You and your family

do not pray to the real God.

You pray to Baal," said Elijah.

"That's why God has not sent rain."

"Bring all the people to the top
of Mount Carmel," said Elijah.

So King Ahab did what Elijah said.

He called all the people together.

They met on the top of the mountain.

Then Elijah said to the people,

"How long are you going to doubt?

Make up your minds!

If God is God then follow him.

If Baal is god, then follow him."

The people did not say a word.

Elijah said, "I am the only one
who still prays to God.
Everyone else prays to Baal.
Let's see who the real God is!
Let's have a contest!"

Elijah said to the people,

"We will each put a bull

on a wooden altar.

You can call on your god.

I will call on my God.

The God who sends fire to the wood

is the true God."

The people liked this idea.

"You can go first," said Elijah.

So the people who prayed to Baal

put a bull on their wooden altar.

Then they called out to Baal

to send fire to the wood.

All morning long they shouted,

"Oh, Baal, answer us!"

But nothing happened.

They shouted louder.

Then they danced around the altar.

But still nothing happened.

In the afternoon Elijah said,

"Maybe your god is asleep.

Maybe he is on a trip.

Shout louder!"

The people cried out to Baal

all day long.

But nothing happened.

When it was late in the day,

they finally gave up.

"Now it's my turn," said Elijah.

Elijah fixed up the Lord's altar,

which had been torn down.

He used twelve stones to fix it.

He dug a trench around it.

He put wood on the altar.

Then he put a bull on the wood.

Elijah told some men,

"Pour four big jars of water

over the wood."

So they poured water over the wood.

"Do it two more times," said Elijah.

So they poured water over the wood two more times.

Water covered the whole altar.

Elijah went to the altar and prayed,
"Oh Lord God, show the people
that you are the true God!"

Then fire came down from heaven!

It burned up the bull and the wood.

It dried up all of the water.

The people cried out,

"The Lord is God!"

Then all the people knew that
Elijah's God was the one true God.
And soon after that,
God sent rain.